SLIP STREAM

DEVIL'S TEETH

STEVE BARLOW AND **STEVE SKIDMORE**
Illustrated by **PAUL MCCAFFREY**

TITLES AT THIS LEVEL

Fiction

FISHING FOR **TROUBLE**
DAVID and HELEN ORME
978 1 4451 1812 3 pb

FOOTBALL **LEGEND**
DAVID and HELEN ORME
978 1 4451 1811 6 pb

VAMPIRES ARE **SO BORING**
DAVID and HELEN ORME
978 1 4451 1813 0 pb

MY NAME IS **COLEN**
STEVE BARLOW and STEVE SKIDMORE
978 1 4451 3070 5 pb

DEVIL'S **TEETH**
STEVE BARLOW and STEVE SKIDMORE
978 1 4451 3054 5 pb

SPACE STATION ALERT
DAVID and HELEN ORME
978 1 4451 3068 2 pb

Graphic fiction

DEMON **STREAK**
JONNY ZUCKER and STEVE SAMPSON
978 1 4451 1799 7 pb

FULL METAL **HERO**
JONNY ZUCKER and DAN BOULTWOOD
978 1 4451 1801 7 pb

TERROR **BEAST**
JONNY ZUCKER and MACK CHATER
978 1 4451 1800 0 pb

ALIEN ACADEMY
JONNY ZUCKER and RYAN PENTNEY
978 1 4451 3088 0 pb

BEYOND THE **WALL**
JONNY ZUCKER and TOMAS ARANDA
978 1 4451 3090 3 pb

DOWNHILL **RACERS**
JONNY ZUCKER and IAIN BUCHANAN
978 1 4451 3089 7 pb

Non-fiction

BIZARRE **BUILDINGS**
ANNE ROONEY
978 1 4451 1952 6 hb
978 1 4451 3229 7 pb

CRAZY **FOOD**
ANNE ROONEY
978 1 4451 1954 0 hb
978 1 4451 3228 0 pb

WACKY **SPORTS**
ANNE ROONEY
978 1 4451 1953 3 hb
978 1 4451 3227 3 pb

AMAZING **PETS**
ANNE ROONEY
978 1 4451 3050 7 hb

DANGEROUS **EARTH**
ANNE ROONEY
978 1 4451 3052 1 hb

WORLD'S **TOUGHEST**
ANNE ROONEY
978 1 4451 3035 4 hb

SLIP STREAM

DEVIL'S TEETH

STEVE BARLOW AND STEVE SKIDMORE
Illustrated by PAUL MCCAFFREY

EDGE
FRANKLIN WATTS
LONDON · SYDNEY

First published in 2014 by
Franklin Watts
338 Euston Road
London NW1 3BH

Franklin Watts Australia
Level 17/207 Kent Street
Sydney NSW 2000

Text © Steve Barlow and Steve Skidmore 2014
Illustration © Franklin Watts 2014

The rights of Steve Barlow and Steve
Skidmore to be identified as the authors of
this Work have been asserted in accordance
with the Copyright, Designs and Patents
Act, 1988.

A CIP catalogue record for this book is
available from the British Library.

(pb) ISBN: 978 1 4451 3054 5
(library ebook) ISBN: 978 1 4451 3057 6

Series Editors: Adrian Cole and Jackie Hamley
Series Advisors: Diana Bentley and Dee Reid
Series Designer: Peter Scoulding

1 3 5 7 9 10 8 6 4 2

Printed in China

Franklin Watts is a division of
Hachette Children's Books,
an Hachette UK company.
www.hachette.co.uk

CONTENTS

CHAPTER 1
A BETTER OFFER

Owen was working on his boat when Emma walked past.

"Do you want to go for a ride?" asked Owen.

Emma looked at the dirty, old boat.

Then Jeb turned up, driving a speedboat.

Jeb waved. "Hi, Emma! Do you want to come for a ride?"

"Cool!" said Emma. "Can Owen come too?"

"OK," said Jeb but he did not look happy.

Owen didn't want to leave Emma alone with Jeb so he got in the boat.

CHAPTER 2
THE DEVIL'S TEETH

"Nice speedboat," said Emma. "Whose boat is it?"

"It's my dad's boat," said Jeb. "Let's go to the Devil's Teeth."

"Bad idea," said Owen. "The Devil's Teeth rocks are dangerous."

The boat raced near the Devil's Teeth.

"Stop it!" snapped Owen. "You will sink us!"

Jeb laughed. "Chicken!"

Owen pointed at the sky. "Take us back.
There is a storm coming."

"Go back?" Jeb frowned. "No way!"

Emma looked scared. "Please, Jeb."

"Oh, all right." Jeb turned the wheel.

A huge wave hit the boat. Jeb flew through the air. He hit his head and was knocked out. The engine died.

CHAPTER 3
STRANDED?

"Look after Jeb," said Owen.

Emma found the boat's first aid kit.

Owen got to work mending the engine.
Five minutes later, the engine roared
into life.

"Look out!" shouted Emma.

Owen looked around in horror.

The boat had drifted into the Devil's Teeth.

"If we hit a rock, we will sink," said Owen.

"I don't know the way out."

CHAPTER 4
A HELPING HAND

"Look over there!" said Emma.

Owen saw an old fishing boat.

On the deck stood an old man holding a lantern.

"He's waving at us to follow him," said Emma.

Carefully, Owen followed the old boat

between the rocks.

CHAPTER 5
RESCUE

"We are through!" cheered Owen.

"But where has the old man gone?" said Emma.

The fishing boat had vanished.

Suddenly Owen and Emma were blinded by a bright searchlight.

"Lifeboat!" came a voice. "Come aboard!"

"You were lucky," said one of the crew. "Those rocks are deadly!"

"An old fisherman showed us the way out," said Owen.

The man stared. "What did this old fisherman look like?"

Owen described the old fisherman and his boat.

"I would like to thank him," said Owen.

"You can't," said the crewman. "That was old Fred Tilly, and his boat was wrecked on the Devil's Teeth thirty years ago. His body was never found."

MY NAME IS
COLEN

STEVE BARLOW AND STEVE SKIDMORE

Colen is not your usual kid next door. When Becca tries to make friends, she knows that things are definitely not right.

Why does he never go out? Why is his uncle so strict?
And why do Colen and his uncle look so similar?

EDGE FRANKLIN WATTS

LONDON•SYDNEY

Space station duty can be boring. But when a direct hit causes
the air supply to fail, Chris and Rob are definitely not bored.
Ground control has been hit by a hurricane so there's no help
on the way from Earth, and they have just 12 hours to try to
save themselves...

EDGE FRANKLIN WATTS

LONDON•SYDNEY

About

SLIPSTREAM

Slipstream is a series of expertly levelled books designed for pupils who are struggling with reading. Its unique three-strand approach through fiction, graphic fiction and non-fiction gives pupils a rich reading experience that will accelerate their progress and close the reading gap.

At the heart of every Slipstream fiction book is a great story. Easily accessible words and phrases ensure that pupils both decode and comprehend, and the high interest stories really engage older struggling readers.

Whether you're using Slipstream Level 2 for Guided Reading or as an independent read, here are some suggestions:

1. Make each reading session successful. Talk about the text before the pupil starts reading. Introduce any unfamiliar vocabulary.

2. Encourage the pupil to talk about the book using a range of open questions. For example, what do they think Emma feels about Jeb at the end of the story?

3. Discuss the differences between reading fiction, graphic fiction and non-fiction. Which do they prefer?

For guidance, SLIPSTREAM Level 2 – Devil's Teeth has been approximately measured to:

National Curriculum Level: 2b

Reading Age: 7.6–8.0

Book Band: Purple

ATOS: 2.0*

Guided Reading Level: I

Lexile® Measure (confirmed): 290L

*Please check actual Accelerated Reader™ book level and quiz availability at www.arbookfind.co.uk